To my family—and yours.
—J.P.T.

To my dear father,
who used to take me for walks
through the cherry blossom tunnels.
—HifuMiyo

Waiting for Hanami
Text copyright © 2025 by Jas Perry
Illustrations copyright © 2025 by HifuMiyo
All rights reserved. Manufactured in Italy.

ISBN 978-0-06-322497-1

The artist used Photoshop to create the digital illustrations for this book.
Typography by Dana Fritts
24 25 26 27 28   RTLO   10 9 8 7 6 5 4 3 2 1
First Edition

Waiting for Hanami

Words by J.P. Takahashi

Art by HifuMiyo

HARPER

An Imprint of HarperCollinsPublishers

When the sakura bloom, it's important to arrive early,
even earlier than the sun . . .

. . . to search for a spot in the park,
right underneath the pink petals.

The one perfect place
for lying down
and looking up.
For hanami.

Sai has been waiting all year—
for the trees' green buds to bloom into pink blossoms,
to see faces she remembers from photos and on screens.
She's here for a big family reunion.

And it's very, very big.

"Last time I saw you, you were *this* small," says a woman with a warm smile.
Long locs swing when her husband leans over. "Pretty soon, you'll be as tall as me!"

The park is buzzing and Sai's heart races.
The puzzle pieces of her world are starting to connect.
Still, Sai feels a tiny bit like a stranger.

But she's not the only one.

Dad says that Avi is a cousin.

No, the cousin of a cousin.

Or maybe an uncle's godson's brother, on Sai's mother's side?

And while they just met, Sai can see what they have in common.

She tells Avi about her parents' kimono shop, where she loves to help out.

When a customer arrives, Sai thinks through her questions carefully.
"If you could live anywhere on earth, where's the first place you'd go?"
"When you were my age, what did you dream about the most?"
And . . .

There! Something lights up in the customer's eyes.
And Sai knows this answer is special.
It has a color and a pattern,
a texture she can almost touch:
peachy rays peeking through the clouds,
a sweet chill in the morning air.

Sai has a kimono in mind.
And when the fit is just right, the sun starts to rise.

The white crane soars
when the belt is tied tight.

It feels like magic, so Sai wisely says,
"This is the one!"
And her job is done.

Avi knows the magic, too.
He *makes* it, using just a notebook and ink.
He imagines whole universes
and all the lives they contain.

His pen climbs high above the clouds
to planets under strange constellations,
dives deep into pitch-black oceans,
where tardy schoolkids swim to class
with glowing gills and slick tails.

His ink runs into a different Avi from another time,
with a better singing voice and a worse haircut.
And it meets Sai from today, when Sai doesn't know what to say.
When she can't explain the tangled feeling and her words slip away,
but Avi's pen can give it a shape.

Sai and Avi both want to recognize familiar faces,
put names to their relatives' voices,
and meet all the new ones, too.
But it's not very easy.
So they do what they know.

Sai thinks through her questions carefully.
She looks for bright eyes and waits for excited answers,
and Avi puts the magic on the page,
connecting all the journeys
their history contains.

Sai asks the family's acrobats and artists
about the truckers and the journalists,
asks the actors and pastors about the athletes and nurses.
Every story reminds her of a pattern, a color,
a texture she can almost touch.

Jumping through time with an easy stroke of his pen,
Avi records memories of laughter and caring and sharing
and the sacred caramel cake recipe you'd be lucky to learn.

When the sakura fall, they won't grow again for a while.
When the family leaves, the next reunion will be far, far away.
But today, the flowers are bright and blooming.
Everyone's here, together—

in one perfect place.

Avi and Sai lie down at last.
The prickly grass tickles their elbows,
and they take a deep breath.
The wait is over.

Finally . . .

. . . they look up.

Author's Note

Hanami, or cherry-blossom viewing, marks the yearly return of the spring season. The tradition began a long time ago in Japan, starting with the emperors and their courts, then continued with the samurai under the rule of the shogun, then, finally, with all the people of Japan. Today we celebrate hanami with Sakura Matsuri—cherry blossom festivals. And everyone is invited.

In the United States, the National Cherry Blossom Festival—the largest in the country—is celebrated in Washington, DC. There are others, too, including San Francisco's festival, where a grand parade follows a route that passes underneath the flowers. Philadelphia showcases performers: martial artists, dancers, drummers, and more. And in New York, the Brooklyn Botanic Garden hosts a Japanese market with treats, crafts, and vintage kimonos.

We wait all year for the flowers to open to the sun. We set our picnics with friends and family, and we look up at the sakura.

Then, only days after blooming, the petals wilt and fall to the ground.

It is beautiful and sorrowful that the cherry blossoms are here and then gone. Their brief lives remind us to appreciate what we have, every day, while we have it.

Saying goodbye is never easy, whether we're parting with the springtime sun or with our favorite cousins at the family reunion. But we can carry the beauty of our new memories with us while we wait. . . .

Until we meet again.